The Boxcar Children Mysteries

The Mystery in New York
The Gymnastics Mystery
The Poison Frog Mystery
The Mystery of the Empty Safe
The Home Run Mystery
The Great Bicycle Race Mystery
The Mystery of the Wild Ponies
The Mystery in the Computer Game
The Honeybee Mystery
The Mystery at the Crooked House
The Hockey Mystery
The Mystery of the Midnight Dog
The Mystery of the Screech Owl
The Summer Camp Mystery
The Copycat Mystery
The Haunted Clock Tower Mystery
The Mystery of the Tiger's Eye
The Disappearing Staircase Mystery
The Mystery on Blizzard Mountain
The Mystery of the Spider's Clue
The Candy Factory Mystery
The Mystery of the Mummy's Curse
The Mystery of the Star Ruby
The Stuffed Bear Mystery
The Mystery of Alligator Swamp
The Mystery at Skeleton Point
The Tattletale Mystery
The Comic Book Mystery
The Great Shark Mystery
The Ice Cream Mystery
The Midnight Mystery
The Mystery in the Fortune Cookie
The Black Widow Spider Mystery
The Radio Mystery
The Mystery of the Runaway Ghost
The Finders Keepers Mystery
The Mystery of the Haunted Boxcar
The Clue in the Corn Maze
The Ghost of the Chattering Bones
The Sword of the Silver Knight
The Game Store Mystery
The Mystery of the Orphan Train
The Vanishing Passenger

The Giant Yo-Yo Mystery
The Creature in Ogopogo Lake
The Rock 'n' Roll Mystery
The Secret of the Mask
The Seattle Puzzle
The Ghost in the First Row
The Box That Watch Found
A Horse Named Dragon
The Great Detective Race
The Ghost at the Drive-In Movie
The Mystery of the Traveling Tomatoes
The Spy Game
The Dog-Gone Mystery
The Vampire Mystery
Superstar Watch
The Spy in the Bleachers
The Amazing Mystery Show
The Pumpkin Head Mystery
The Cupcake Caper
The Clue in the Recycling Bin
Monkey Trouble
The Zombie Project
The Great Turkey Heist
The Garden Thief
The Boardwalk Mystery
The Mystery of the Fallen Treasure
The Return of the Graveyard Ghost
The Mystery of the Stolen Snowboard
The Mystery of the Wild West Bandit
The Mystery of the Grinning Gargoyle
The Mystery of the Soccer Snitch
The Mystery of the Missing Pop Idol
The Mystery of the Stolen Dinosaur Bones
The Mystery at the Calgary Stampede
The Sleepy Hollow Mystery
The Legend of the Irish Castle
The Celebrity Cat Caper
Hidden in the Haunted School
The Election Day Dilemma

HIDDEN IN THE HAUNTED SCHOOL

created by
GERTRUDE CHANDLER WARNER

Illustrated by Anthony VanArsdale

Albert Whitman & Company
Chicago, Illinois

Library of Congress Cataloging-in-Publication
data is on file with the publisher.

Copyright © 2016 by Albert Whitman & Company
Published in 2016 by Albert Whitman & Company

ISBN 978-0-8075-0718-6 (hardcover)
ISBN 978-0-8075-0719-3 (paperback)

Printed in the United States of America
10 9 8 7 6 5 4 3 2 1 LB 20 19 18 17 16

THE BOXCAR CHILDREN® is a registered
trademark of Albert Whitman & Company.

Illustrated by Anthony VanArsdale

For more information about Albert Whitman & Company,
visit our web site at www.albertwhitman.com.

Contents

CHAPTER 1

Ghost Stories

Crunch! Benny Alden took a big bite out of his crisp, red apple as he sat in the backseat of the family's minivan. It was a late-fall Saturday, and he and his brother and sisters had helped their grandfather run errands in Silver City, the town next to Greenfield. They'd made a lot of stops, including at the farmers' market. Benny, who was six years old and always hungry, was munching on his second apple, which he'd retrieved from one of the bags of fresh fruits and vegetables tucked near

1

his seat. Now it was late afternoon, and the Aldens were headed home.

Twelve-year-old Jessie put her hand on the cool glass of the minivan's window. She watched trees with red, orange, and yellow leaves whiz by. She thought the leaves looked even prettier than usual in the setting sun. Just then, she remembered the notebook in her backpack. She pulled it out and opened it to check the list of errands they'd made that day. She liked making lists and used her organizational skills to help her family.

"Grandfather," Jessie called to the front seat. "I think we forgot to pick up the dry cleaning."

"You're right!" her grandfather replied. He clicked on the turn signal and turned the van down a side street. "It's a bit out of the way, but I think I know a shortcut to the cleaners."

Benny looked around the minivan.

"I don't think we have room for one more thing," he said. "It's crowded in here!" He was sitting next to Violet, his ten-year-old sister, who was busy doodling with her favorite purple pen in her sketch pad. They were surrounded by bags and boxes holding everything the Aldens had bought or picked up on their errands.

"We'll make room," Henry told his little brother. At fourteen, Henry was the oldest of the Alden children. He sat in the front seat, tinkering with the radio. "Watch can sit on your lap!"

Watch, the Aldens' terrier, replied with a small yap—as if he knew everyone was talking about him. They all laughed as the dog jumped into Benny's lap and curled into a ball.

A few miles and a couple of turns later, the minivan drove down a narrow road that ran along the edge of town. The street was very quiet. The children didn't see any other cars, just rows and rows of trees in the woods on either side of them.

"What's that?" Benny asked, pointing out his window. The Alden children turned to see an old brick building surrounded by a black iron fence. The fence had spiked posts, and overgrown vines hung from the roof. Henry looked beyond the locked gate to read the letters carved into the stone above the entrance.

"Hawthorne School," he said. "I've heard stories about it."

The dark shadows behind the school's broken windows made Violet shiver in her seat.

A few minutes later, Grandfather drove the minivan into the lot of Silver City Plaza, a shopping center with half a dozen stores. The spots in front of the dry cleaning shop were full, so he parked in front of Weaver's Flower Shop.

"I'll be right back," he told his grandchildren.

Grandfather had been gone only a moment when Benny spoke up. "Tell us about Hawthorne School," he said to his brother. "It looks spooky."

"Do you mean Haunted School?" Henry asked. "That's what they call it."

"Why?" Violet asked. Although she certainly thought the school looked haunted.

"Well, it's been abandoned since the 1950s," Henry said. "The gates haven't been opened since the day it closed."

"That doesn't make it haunted," Violet pointed out.

"Of course not," Jessie agreed. "But now that you mention it, wasn't the ghost story we heard last weekend about this school?"

Last weekend, Grandfather had treated Henry, Jessie, and a few of their friends to a campfire. Violet and Benny had stayed in the house to watch a movie with Mrs. McGregor. As the group sat around the small fire pit, they roasted marshmallows and exchanged their scariest ghost stories. Jessie's friend, Rose, had told everyone the tale of a haunted school—a school that she said was nearby. It had to be Hawthorne School.

Henry nodded. "I remember. The story says the ghost of the former principal still walks the halls of the school."

"A *ghost*?" Benny asked.

"That's right," Jessie said, recalling the story. "She was fired from her job because a teacher reported that she was stealing money from the school. After weeks of insisting she didn't do it, the principal was still told to leave. As she walked out of the building, she put a curse on the school!"

"The money was later found," Henry continued. "It turns out she didn't steal it after all."

"Did she get her job back?" Benny asked.

"No," Jessie replied. "Nobody could find her after she was asked to leave. She seemed to just...vanish."

"Now," Henry added, "if you look through the old windows, you can see her walking back and forth through the halls. Or that's what they say, at least."

"Wow!" Benny exclaimed.

"A real ghost!" Violet said.

"We don't really believe the story," Henry said. "It's probably just a local legend."

The Alden children looked at one another, deep in thought. They heard the clicking sound of the door being unlocked and turned their attention back to Grandfather. He had returned from the dry cleaners with an armload of plastic-covered shirts.

"Look what I found," he said, climbing into the minivan. He handed a yellow piece of paper to Jessie. "You might want to consider this for service work."

Jessie read the paper. She smiled and handed it to Henry.

"Volunteers needed," he read aloud. "Thanks, Grandfather!"

Henry and Jessie's middle school required them to work ten hours of community service every year. In return, they received extra credit. They both enjoyed helping in the neighborhood and meeting new people, and they were looking for new places to volunteer.

"I was thinking about helping the teachers at Greenfield Day Care Center," Jessie said as Grandfather started the car on the journey home. "They can always use an extra pair of hands."

"And the Rec Center is looking for junior camp leaders," Henry added. "Taking little kids on adventures would be fun!"

Benny looked out the window and into the woods as they drove past them again. He thought about his own exciting adventure.

Years ago, the children's parents had died, leaving them without a home. They knew they had a grandfather but had never met him, and they had heard he was mean. So, when they thought they would be sent to live with him, they ran away into the woods. There they found an old boxcar, which they made their home. They found their dog, Watch, while they were living in the boxcar. When Grandfather finally discovered the children, they learned he was actually a very kind man. He loved them very much. They became a family, and Grandfather moved their boxcar into the backyard of their home in Greenfield so they could use it as a clubhouse.

"I wish I could help with the little kids," Benny said. The Aldens laughed, since Benny was not much older than the campers.

"It would be great to find a place where we could all work together," Jessie added.

"Any other ideas?" Grandfather asked.

The Aldens were quiet for a moment as they tried to think of places where they could all volunteer as a family.

Suddenly Violet gasped. "Stop!" she cried. "Look!"

Grandfather pulled the car over to the side of the road.

"What's the matter, Violet?" he asked.

They were sitting in front of Hawthorne School.

Violet pointed a shaky finger out the window.

"The door to the school is open!" she exclaimed. "It wasn't before!"

The Aldens peered out to see that the iron gate of the old school was wide open. And so was the front door!

"I thought the school has been locked up since it closed," Benny said.

"It has been," Henry replied.

The siblings looked at the old school. The sun was setting behind the trees, casting a long shadow across the front of the building. In the darkness, the children could clearly see a flickering light in one of the upstairs windows.

"Is someone in there?" Violet asked. "Is this school really haunted?"

Chapter 2

The Old Becomes New

"Well, would you look at that," Grandfather marveled. "Nobody's been in that place for over fifty years. I wonder what's happening."

"Do you think it's haunted?" Benny asked.

"I saw a light flickering!" Violet said.

"So did I," Jessie added. "Look through the upstairs window!"

Through the window, everyone saw a dim flicker of light. Then, the school went dark again.

"Wait," said Henry. "I think I know what's

going on."

He unfolded the yellow piece of paper that Grandfather had given them. "I saw something on this flyer, and now it all makes sense." He read the flyer over before reading it aloud.

"'Volunteers needed,'" he began. "'For a renovation project and cleanup at the new Hawthorne Art Center.'"

"That's right," Grandfather said, scratching his chin. "I remember reading something about this in the *Greenfield Gazette*. Silver City has been planning to fix up an old building for their art center. They must have picked the old Hawthorne School."

"A community art center?" Violet asked. "I wonder what art programs they'll offer." She motioned for Jessie to hand her the flyer. "Art and dance classes," she read aloud from the paper. "And, they will have a theater for plays and music recitals!"

"What a nice addition to Silver City," Grandfather said.

"I really want to know more!" Jessie agreed.

Henry looked up at the old school, imagining how the building would look when it was fixed up. He noticed a rusty blue pickup in the school's parking lot. The truck had a ladder and a big toolbox in the back. *Silver City Electric* was written on the truck's side in silver letters. Henry pointed it out to his siblings.

"That truck looks familiar," he said.

"As a matter of fact, that's my old friend Bob's truck," Grandfather told them. "Remember when he fixed the lights at our house? He's an electrician here in town."

"That's right," Henry said. "Will he know about the restoration project?"

"We should ask him!" Violet said. As shy as she was, she was the one who was the most excited about the new art center.

"Sure," Grandfather replied. "I've known Bob for years. It will be good to catch up with him."

"Do you think the school is as creepy on the inside as it is on the outside?" Jessie asked.

"I hope so!" Benny said.

Jessie slid the minivan door open.

"Come on, Watch!" Benny called. Watch trotted happily alongside the Aldens as they made their way past the iron fence and gate.

As they approached the stone front steps, Bob stepped into the doorway and waved. "Hello!" he called.

He wore a blue and silver T-shirt with *Silver City Electric* on it and carried a flashlight. He stepped out onto the stairs and closed the school door behind him.

Grandfather waved back. "Hi, Bob! We saw your truck. Do you remember my grandchildren?"

Bob greeted Henry, Jessie, Violet, and Benny, giving each a friendly handshake. Suddenly, the school's door swung open with a loud *clank*. A young man appeared. He was wearing a T-shirt like Bob's. His sandy-brown hair matched Bob's too. He held a large camera that hung from a brown leather strap around his neck.

"There you are, Ansel," Bob said to the young man. "I must have lost you inside." He introduced the young man as his son. Ansel gave them a quick wave before turning away and fiddling with his camera.

"We must've seen your flashlight!" Henry said. He remembered the light they saw flickering in the window.

"I'm sure you did," Bob replied. "Ansel and I just stopped by to look at the old place. I'm overseeing the renovation project and need to make sure it's safe for our volunteers. The inside isn't too bad, just needs a little elbow grease."

Jessie's eyes grew wide, and so did her smile. "Bob," she started. "Are you still looking for volunteers?"

"We'd love to help," Violet added. She didn't want to miss an opportunity to work on the new art center.

"We sure could use volunteers," Bob replied. "We'd love for every one of you to pitch in." He nodded to all of the Alden children.

"Can you tell me more about the project?" Grandfather asked.

He then pulled Bob aside to ask about the specific jobs his grandchildren would be doing.

While Grandfather and Bob were talking, Ansel was still busy with his camera, staring at the digital screen. He carefully studied each photo as he clicked through them.

"Will you also be working here, Ansel?" Henry asked.

"I'm on the arts committee," Ansel replied, though he didn't look up from his camera. "So, I'll be around."

"Let's look inside," Benny suggested. He pointed to the grand door of the school. "Just a peek!"

"First," Henry said, "let's ask Bob if it's safe."

Grandfather gave his approval with a brief thumbs-up gesture.

"Grandfather agrees with Bob," Henry said. "The structure is safe."

"Let's go!" Benny said.

Henry opened the school's door. Jessie found a large stone and propped the door open with it.

"Come on, Watch!" she called.

Inside, Violet instantly noticed a trophy case. It was covered with a layer of soot, dust, and grime. A few trophies remained in the case. Through the dirty glass, Violet saw a tall, tarnished old cup. On another shelf, smaller trophies were draped in cobwebs. She frowned.

"At one time," she said, pointing to the trophies, "these were shiny and new."

The Aldens continued walking along the dark hallway.

"Check this out," Jessie said. She was peering at a framed black-and-white photo hanging on the wall. The picture was faded and torn around the edges. The students in the picture wore dark, formal clothes. The date *March 14, 1920* was scribbled on the bottom. Jessie recorded the date in her notebook.

"They're not smiling," Henry noted.

"I don't think it was fashionable to smile in pictures back then," Jessie replied.

Benny followed his sisters and brother as they walked into a classroom. The first thing he noticed was a large clock on the wall behind an old teacher's desk. The clock's hands had stopped with the hour hand pointing to twelve and the minute hand to three. Benny shuddered. He wondered how long ago the clock's hands had stopped turning.

"This place is definitely as creepy on the inside as the outside!" he exclaimed.

Rows of smaller desks sat across from the teacher's desk. Jessie lifted one of the desks' tops. Inside, she found broken pencils and old papers. Shifting through the papers, Violet found an old cloth doll. The doll's hair was made of yellow yarn, and its clothes were faded fabric scraps. A small button had been sewn on for an eye, but the other eye's button was missing.

"This place *is* spooky," Violet said. "We'd better get back. Grandfather might be looking for us."

When the Aldens returned to the front steps, Grandfather was still talking with Bob.

"Good news," Grandfather said. "Volunteers start next week."

"We'll get this place looking brand-new!" Bob said.

"Sure," Ansel muttered.

He kept his head down, but it looked to Jessie like he was trying to hide a scowl.

She wondered why Ansel wasn't more excited to be a part of the project. After all, it

was an art center, and he clearly loved taking photos.

"We're going to grab the volunteer paperwork from the truck," Grandfather said. He and Bob headed toward the parking lot.

While they all waited, Ansel sighed. He looked unhappy.

Jessie tried to break the ice. "Are you excited about the new art center?"

Ansel looked up. Then he turned and gazed up at the old school. His eyes narrowed. "This place should be kept the way it is," he said bitterly. And with that, he marched off to the parking lot.

"What was that about?" Henry asked.

Jessie shrugged. "I don't know," she said.

"I want to see the swings!" Benny said just then. He had noticed the rusty playground equipment near the front fence. "Can we wait for Grandfather on the playground?"

"Sure," Jessie said. "But be careful." They walked over to the broken-down playground. Violet and Benny sat on the swings, which creaked and screeched as they moved back and forth. They faced the school yard where the grass and shrubs were overgrown. Long vines wrapped around the fence. The untended yard added to the creepiness of the school.

Henry walked around looking at the old seesaws, while Jessie sat still on one of the swings. She was thinking about Ansel's odd behavior. Her thoughts were interrupted by Watch's loud bark, which startled her.

"What's with Watch?" Benny asked. The dog had tensed up, and now he nervously paced in front of the children. Then he stopped and growled in the direction of the school.

"It feels like...like someone is watching us," Jessie said.

Benny looked at the dark windows of the old school. "There's no such thing as ghosts," he said aloud. "Right?"

Chapter 3

An Important Lesson

It was the first day of volunteer work.

"See you in a few hours!" Grandfather called from the minivan. He waved to the children as they climbed the front steps of Hawthorne School.

Jessie stopped for a moment to look up at the old building. In the morning daylight, Jessie couldn't remember what about the place had her so nervous just a week ago.

"Hawthorne School doesn't look so spooky today," Violet said. She was thinking the same thing as her sister.

So was Henry, who gazed at the tower on the top of the school. It looked majestic against the clear, sunny sky.

Today the school wasn't deserted at all. Two dozen volunteers had come to help clean up the building. Benny thought all the people looked like a swarm of worker ants. Some were carrying buckets and brooms. They busily swept the sidewalks and stairs. Other volunteers had paintbrushes tucked into their back pockets. Henry stepped off the sidewalk to let two men carrying a faded sofa go by. He had moved just in time. Two more volunteers went by carrying an old rolled-up rug.

The inside of the school was just as busy. A team of teens from the high school was washing the thick grime from windows. Nearby, a group of women was scraping the windowsills clean to prepare them for a fresh coat of paint.

After a few minutes, the Aldens found Bob at the volunteer check-in table. He checked their names off a long list and then gave the children their assignments.

"Benny and Violet," Bob said. "You will be helping hand out water and snacks at the snack tent on the front lawn."

"Perfect!" Benny exclaimed.

"Just don't eat all the snacks," Violet added. Everyone laughed, including Benny.

Bob turned to Henry and Jessie. "You'll be sweeping and dusting classrooms today."

"Great," Henry said.

Meanwhile Jessie looked around and noticed a large sign in the corner that said AUCTION. She was curious.

"What's the auction?" she asked Bob.

"The volunteers will bring the old furniture up here." He pointed to the corner. "We'll evaluate it. And then we'll sell it in an auction. The money we make will cover some of the renovation costs."

Everyone agreed an auction was a great idea. They headed back outside and found the snack table. It was set up under a large, blue tent. Benny and Violet went to work placing bottles of water on a table.

"We'll be right inside," Jessie told them.

Henry and Jessie stopped to pick up

brooms and dusting cloths before heading back into the school. After sweeping the main hallway, they started working in one of the old classrooms.

Henry pulled a cloth out of his back pocket. With a swipe of his hand, he removed a thick layer of grime from a window. When he finished one window, he moved on to the next one.

"It will take some elbow grease to get these windows clean," he said.

Jessie wrinkled her nose as she used her broom to pull a stringy cobweb from the corner. Then she swept a big pile of dust bunnies into a dustpan. She was finishing up when a young woman walked into the classroom. The woman had dark hair with bangs that fell into her eyes.

"Hi," Jessie said, walking over to her. "I'm Jessie. And this is my brother, Henry."

"Hello," the woman replied. "I'm Martha."

Martha immediately began to follow Jessie and Henry around the room with a cloth rag in her hand. Every once in a while, she wiped the rag over the top of a desk or along the seat of a chair.

Henry noticed that Martha was missing spots. She seemed to be focused on studying the furniture, rather than dusting it. He watched her lift a chair and inspect the bottom of it. She even examined the legs of a table.

"These chairs are in good shape for being so old," Martha muttered.

Henry agreed. "Will you be working here all weekend?" he asked.

Martha seemed a little flustered by his question.

"Yes," she replied. "I'll be here with you and your brother and sisters. How's your little dog, Watch? Is he here today too?"

"No," Henry replied. "He's at home."

Jessie was still sweeping when she overheard Martha talking with Henry. She wondered how Martha knew their dog's name. Jessie was certain that this was their first time meeting her.

But before she had a chance to ask Martha about it, another woman wandered into the room. Her gray hair was braided and wrapped in a bun. She wore glasses on a chain around her neck. She took several moments to carefully review the room.

"Did I leave my clipboard in here?" the woman asked. "I'm supposed to be counting the desks and chairs, but I can't seem to find my clipboard."

The woman looked confused.

"We'll help you find it!" Jessie offered.

"Thank you, dear," the woman replied. She lifted her glasses, still glancing around the room. "I'm Mrs. Koslowski. But you can call me Mrs. K."

Jessie and Henry introduced themselves. Then they propped their brooms against the wall. As they walked out of the classroom, Henry turned to Martha.

"It was nice meeting you, Martha," Henry said. "See you around."

Mumbling a few words of farewell, Martha went back to dusting off a file cabinet.

"Where were you last working?" Henry asked as they walked down the hallway.

"Well, I was in one of the classrooms," Mrs. K replied. "But I can't remember which one."

Just then, Jessie noticed Ansel leaning against the stairwell banister. His eyes were focused on his camera.

"Hello, Ansel!" Mrs. K called. "Have you been here long?"

Ansel looked up and gave a fast wave.

"No," he replied. "Just arrived." And then

he went back to looking at his camera. He was no more excited to be here than the day the Aldens had met him.

Henry was surprised that Mrs. K was so forgetful but had remembered Ansel's name. He figured the two had met each other earlier, so he didn't give it much more thought.

As they turned a corner, they heard excited voices coming from down the hall.

"It sounds like something is happening in Room 107," Henry said, pointing to a nearby classroom.

"We better check it out," Jessie replied. "Do you mind if we make a quick stop, Mrs. K?"

Mrs. Koslowski shook her head and followed Jessie and Henry into the room. They saw several volunteers huddled around a chalkboard, along with two of the handymen who were doing the heavier work around the school.

"What's going on?" Jessie asked.

One of the handymen pointed to a large, old bulletin board that had been taken off the wall. "When we removed this," he replied, "we found an even older chalkboard underneath!" He pointed to the chalkboard on the wall. It was clearly much older than the others in the classroom. It had cracks and plaster around the edges, since it had been hidden in the wall underneath the bulletin board. But the most remarkable thing about it was that the chalkboard still had writing and pictures on it!

The handyman explained that some of the classrooms had been redecorated a long time ago. Many years ago, builders had put up walls and bulletin boards right on top of the old chalkboards. "You know how sometimes in an old house you'll peel back the wallpaper and find older wallpaper underneath? It's a little like that," he said. "We've found old chalkboards in the other rooms, but as you can see, this one is special."

Jessie could see why. The old chalkboard had never been erased after the last time it was used. It was filled with lessons and drawings from nearly one hundred years ago!

"Look at this," Henry exclaimed, pointing to a corner of the chalkboard. "The date is March 20, 1920!"

Everyone gathered around to study the old chalk writing. There was a lesson about a classic poem, which read:

How doth the little busy bee
Improve each shining hour,
And gather honey all the day
From every opening flower!

Henry didn't recognize the poem, but he did admire the old-fashioned cursive handwriting used to write it. Next to the poem was a drawing of a little girl wearing a long dress. It looked like something that would have been stylish many years ago.

Jessie looked at the old arithmetic tables that had been drawn up in one corner. "It's like the students' work has been captured in time!" she marveled.

"This reminds me of my mother's fancy handwriting," Mrs. Koslowski said, coming closer to the chalkboard. "Beautiful penmanship like this isn't taught anymore."

More volunteers came into the classroom as word caught on about the old chalkboard, and they all chatted excitedly about the discovery.

Jessie noticed Ansel walking into the classroom. He snapped a few quick photos, then quietly slipped out of the room.

As he left, Martha strolled in. She looked over the old chalkboard but didn't join in the conversation.

"We should contact the *Silver City Herald*," a young woman suggested. "I'm sure the newspaper will be fascinated by this lesson in history!"

Suddenly, Martha seemed very interested in the volunteers' conversation. She walked over and sat down with the group.

"The newspaper will *not* be interested in this," Martha said. She pulled a notebook from her bag and scribbled down a few notes.

"It's so interesting!" one of the volunteers called out.

"We should not call the local news," Martha repeated.

Jessie watched. She thought that Martha muttered something else under her breath, but she couldn't make out the words. All she knew was that Martha looked irritated. *Why?* Jessie wondered.

Just then, a red-haired girl ran into the classroom. She looked pale and was out of breath.

"Something's wrong next door!" she said.

CHAPTER 4

The Locked Door

Jessie and Henry rushed into the hall with the other volunteers. The red-haired girl stood in front of Room 108. With a shaky finger, she pointed to the door.

"What's wrong?" Jessie asked.

The girl's face reddened as she struggled to explain. "I-I was sweeping in there when I realized I forgot my dustpan," she started. "I left the room for just a minute to get it."

She paused to take a deep breath. Jessie could see that the girl was not only baffled, but frightened.

"I heard the door slam shut," the girl continued. "When I came back, the door was locked!"

By now a small crowd had gathered. Even Benny and Violet had come in from the snack table to see what was going on.

A few volunteers tried to open the door. Benny went over and pulled on the knob too. But the door was definitely locked.

"Maybe the wind blew it closed," suggested one volunteer.

"Or, someone else closed and locked the door," offered another.

After a few moments, a woman stepped forward to speak to the crowd. She nervously twirled the cord of her name tag.

"I'm a coordinator on this project," she said. "And I know for a fact that the doors only lock from inside the classroom."

"Is somebody in there?" Henry asked.

"I don't think so," replied the coordinator. "We've got someone bringing a ladder to look in the room and check." She pointed to a small, high window above the door.

The group became noisy as everyone tried to offer explanations for the locked door.

A burly man from the construction crew pushed through the group carrying a ladder. He smiled as he leaned the ladder against the wall next to the door.

"I'll get to the bottom of this," he said. He climbed the ladder. Then he peered into the small window. By the time he turned to face the group, his smile had faded.

"The room is empty," he said in amazement as he climbed back down the ladder. Then he tested the door to make sure it really was locked. The door remained tightly shut.

Henry exchanged a look with Jessie. Something strange was happening, and they had to see for themselves.

"If you don't mind, may I take a look?" Harry asked the burly man.

"Be my guest," the man replied. "Maybe you'll see something I missed."

Henry climbed up the ladder and peeked through the window. Scanning the room, he realized that nothing unusual stood out. There was definitely nobody in the room, either.

"It's empty," he confirmed.

One of the volunteers gasped in astonishment. Another nervously hugged her arms to her chest.

"Was it a...*ghost* who locked the room?" the red-haired girl asked. "Is the school really haunted?"

The volunteer coordinator stepped forward again.

"It's getting late," she announced. "We'll try to resolve this tomorrow. For now, let's all head home."

Everyone gathered their belongings and shuffled out of the school. On their way out, the volunteers exchanged tales about the Hawthorne ghost. They wondered if the old principal was still walking the halls...and locking classroom doors.

***

"What's going on?" Violet asked. "There are ghost rumors everywhere. Even at the snack tent!"

"Really?" Jessie said.

Violet nodded. "We were handing out water when one of the volunteers asked us about the furniture."

"The furniture?" Henry asked. "What about it?"

"It's been moved!" Benny said.

"That's right," Violet added. "Apparently, some of the furniture was found in the basement."

"And," Benny continued, "nobody knows how it got there."

The Aldens headed toward the parking lot. When they arrived, they spotted Grandfather talking with Bob.

"Bob was just telling me some good news!" Grandfather said when they reached the minivan.

"What's happening?" Violet asked. Everything that involved the art center excited her.

"The arts committee has decided to throw a grand opening party," Bob said. "It's scheduled for six weeks from today. And you are all invited!"

"That's great!" Henry said.

Grandfather nodded. "It's a nice way to let the community know about the new art center."

"It's a tight deadline," Bob said. "But we can do it!"

"Sure!" Grandfather agreed. "Just stay on track, and everything will be ready in time for the party!"

The Aldens climbed into the minivan while discussing the plans for the grand opening. After waving farewell to Bob, Grandfather drove toward Greenfield.

"How was work today?" he asked. "Do you think the art center will be ready in time for the party?"

Violet frowned. She thought about all of the spooky things that had happened that day.

"The school might be haunted," she finally replied.

"Why do you think that?" Grandfather asked.

Violet and the others told him what had happened.

"I'm sure there are reasonable explanations," Grandfather told her.

"I hope it's not haunted," Violet added. "The art center is going to be great!"

As they continued driving, Jessie flipped through the pages of her notebook. She didn't believe in ghosts. But it was clear from her notes that something strange was happening at Hawthorne School. Jessie wondered why Martha had been so irritated when the volunteers mentioned contacting the newspaper. Then there was Room 108. How could the door be locked from the inside when the room was empty?

Benny distracted her from her thoughts. "Something smells good!" he said. He looked around and pulled out a paper bag. WEAVER'S FLOWER AND GARDEN SHOP was written on it in colorful letters. When Benny opened the bag, an aroma of fresh herbs floated into the minivan.

"Weaver's had a special on herbs," Grandfather explained. "I think I'll make my famous spaghetti soon!"

"That is a very good idea!" Benny replied.

Everyone giggled. But as excited as they were about Grandfather's delicious spaghetti, they were also troubled. The day's events had been very unusual. The Aldens rode the rest of the way home in silence. They were busy thinking about how the door to Room 108 could be locked.

***

Grandfather dropped them off at Hawthorne School early the next morning. The first thing the children did was go to the door of Room 108. They found volunteers gathered there. Now the door was wide open! Everyone was curious.

"Did someone unlock the door?" Benny asked.

"No!" the volunteer coordinator replied. "It was just...open when we got here."

Jessie spotted Martha standing next to Mrs. Koslowski.

"Good morning," Jessie said.

But Martha and Mrs. K didn't hear Jessie. They were too busy discussing the Hawthorne School ghost.

"Do you think it's the ghost of the principal?" Martha asked.

"What if the uncovered chalkboard upset her?" Mrs. K continued.

"We shouldn't have moved anything,"

another volunteer added.

"I also heard that furniture has been turning up in odd places," another volunteer continued. "Bob said that some of the old desks were in the basement."

"Really?" Martha asked. "Bob noticed the furniture had been moved?"

"Yes," the volunteer confirmed. "And he doesn't know how it got there."

Jessie thought Martha had a strange expression on her face. She seemed uneasy, but she didn't say anything else.

"Maybe the locked door was a sign that the Hawthorne ghost doesn't want to be disturbed," Mrs. K suggested.

Jessie stepped back and motioned to her brothers and sister to follow her.

"What's going on?" Violet asked, once they were away from the crowd.

"Let's find a private place to talk," Jessie suggested.

They followed her down the hallway. Just as they turned a corner, they saw a glimpse of a figure quickly ducking into a classroom.

"Was that Ansel?" Henry asked.

"It sure looked like him," Violet said. "Where did he go?"

"Why isn't he helping the volunteers?" Jessie asked.

Henry shrugged.

"He's very mysterious," he replied.

They continued until they reached a set of swinging double doors.

Jessie peeked through a small crack between the doors.

"It's the gym!" she said. "Let's sit down in here."

Benny swung open the doors and rushed through them.

"Wow," he said. "I've never been in here before."

The gym floor was grubby and strewn with old leaves that had blown in through one of the broken windows, but even so, the Aldens could see the gym floor still had some of its old shine. Instead of being spooky, the big room was bright and pleasant, with the sunlight coming through the grimy skylights overhead.

"It's just like our gym at school!" Jessie exclaimed. "Only dustier."

"That's for sure," Henry said.

Tattered nets hung from the basketball hoops. The scoreboard looked broken, and the leather mats hanging along the wall were stiff and cracked. Paint peeled from the bleachers, which looked too rickety to sit on. But there was a pair of low, sturdy benches by the door.

"Let's sit down," Jessie suggested.

The Aldens sat facing one another on the wood benches.

"Something strange is definitely happening around here," Jessie said. "Did you hear about the desks that showed up in the basement? A couple of the volunteers were talking about them."

"Maybe Bob moved them?" Henry suggested.

"That's the thing," Jessie continued. "I just heard the volunteers say that Bob doesn't know how they got there. Nobody does."

Violet shivered. "Everyone thinks it's the ghost, don't they?"

"Well," Jessie said. "Martha looked upset when she heard about the furniture in the basement. But I'm not sure what that means."

"Maybe it means she believes in the Hawthorne School ghost," Violet said.

"But there's no such thing as ghosts," Benny said. "Right?"

"Right!" Henry replied.

"So who's causing all of the strange things to happen?" Benny asked.

"That's what we have to figure out." Henry replied.

The children looked around the gym. Even though it wasn't spooky like the rest of the school, there were so many unanswered questions.

Henry stood up. "Let's get to work," he suggested. "There's still a lot to do before the grand opening."

"And today, we have granola bars at the snack tent!" Benny added.

Everyone laughed as they got up and walked out of the gym. When they were back in the hallway, Jessie stopped to face her brothers and sister.

"There may not be a ghost," she said. "But

we should all keep an eye out for anything unusual."

As they were about to head to their jobs, they head a sharp cry that stopped them short. The noise had come from above them.

"What was *that*?" Violet asked.

"That," Jessie said, "was a scream!"

CHAPTER 5

A Mysterious Warning

"Let's go," Henry said. He pointed to the floor above them. "It's coming from upstairs!"

When the Aldens reached the second floor, they heard voices coming from Room 214. They went into the room, where a group of volunteers—including Martha and Mrs. K—were talking nervously. A few of the volunteers looked pale and frightened.

"What's going on?" Henry asked. "We heard someone scream."

The volunteers were huddled in the front

of the classroom. Martha stepped aside so the Alden children could see the chalkboard. She waved at it, motioning for them to step forward for a closer look. When they did, they saw a message written on it. The cursive handwriting looked very much like the writing found on the old hidden chalkboard in Room 107. The same fancy handwriting that Mrs. K had admired.

"What does it mean?" Jessie asked. She opened her notebook and wrote down the exact words of the message.

Stay away! Whoever dares unlock my secret will be sorry!

She wondered who would send such a warning.

"When I was working in here earlier, the chalkboard was blank!" Martha explained. She took a few deep breaths before she continued. "I stepped away for just a few minutes to get a bottle of water from the snack tent. When I returned…I saw the message!"

Martha shivered.

"It must be the ghost," she said nervously.

One of the volunteers, an older lady with

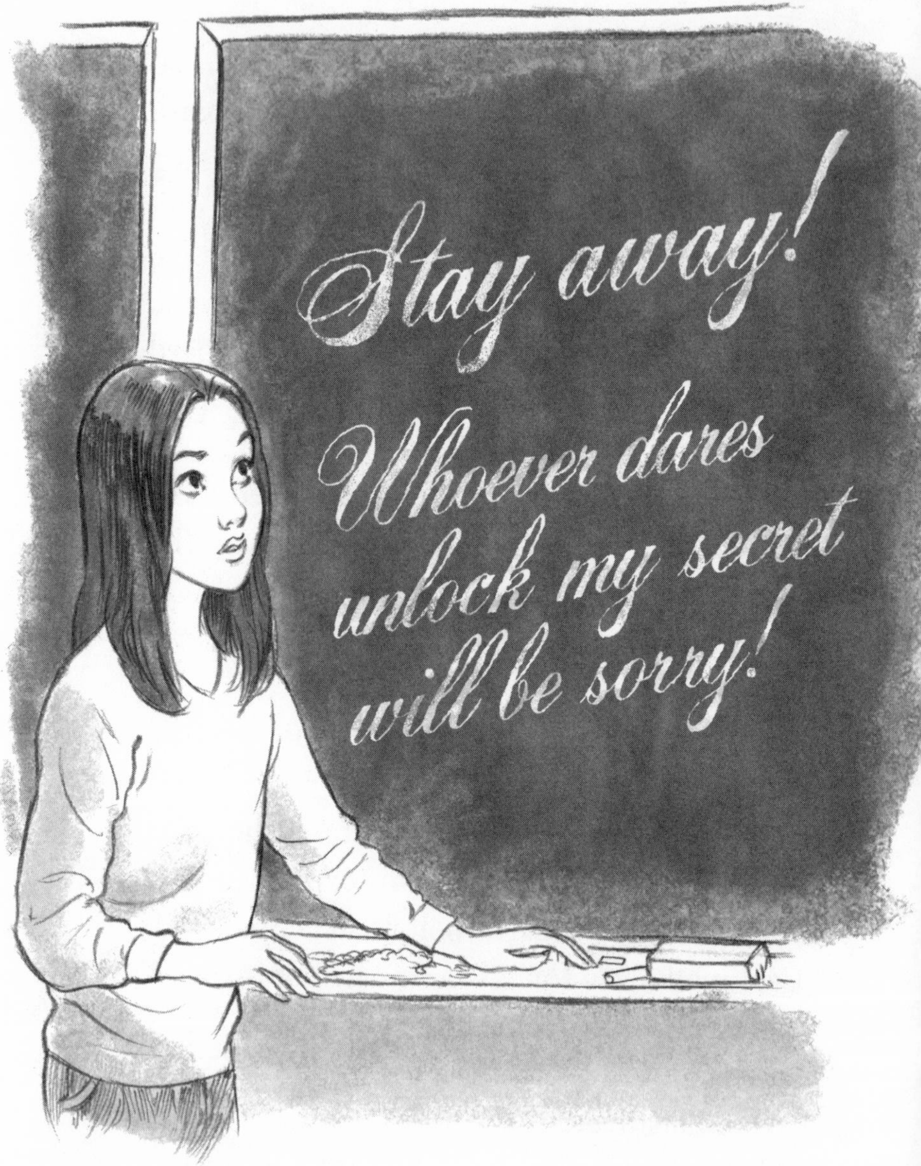
Stay away!
Whoever dares
unlock my secret
will be sorry!

graying curls, was also visibly shaken by the eerie message. She stared at the chalkboard and blinked several times. She seemed to be trying to convince herself that she was really seeing the strange words.

"The legend must be true," she finally said. "The Hawthorne School ghost doesn't want us here!"

For a few more moments, she continued to gaze at the chalkboard. And then suddenly, she began collecting her bags and belongings.

"I'm not sticking around to find out what's going on here," she said as she slipped on her jacket. Swinging her bag over her shoulder, she marched out of the classroom.

A short woman with blond hair had been watching the group. She abruptly stood up from her chair. "I think I'll join her," she said. She gave an apologetic glance as she left the room.

Another volunteer started to gather his belongings. "I don't believe in ghosts," he said. "But this is very strange!" He rushed out the door.

The Alden children looked at one another.

If many more volunteers left, the art center wouldn't be finished in time for the grand opening. Everyone seemed shaken by the message. But the Aldens knew that time was ticking. They had to find out who was behind this…and fast!

"I'm sure a ghost isn't responsible for this message," Jessie said. She remembered her grandfather's advice. "There must be a reasonable answer."

She looked over at the remaining volunteers, who were still staring at the message and talking among themselves. Martha looked uneasy. She put a hand against the wall to steady herself, and Jessie thought that she might faint.

"Are you OK?" Jessie asked. She jumped out of her seat so Martha could sit down.

"Thanks," Martha replied. "Would you mind handing me my bottle of water? It's over there in my bag." She pointed to a large leather tote bag sitting on the window ledge.

"Sure," Jessie said. She went over to the bag and looked inside. There she saw a box of business cards that had accidentally opened up. A dozen identical bright-green cards had spilled out and were scattered all throughout the bag. Jessie could see they were Martha's business cards, and as she pulled out the water bottle she couldn't help but read one that was facing up.

Jessie quickly closed the bag, then went over to Martha and handed her the water.

"Thank you," Martha replied, still sounding a little upset.

"I hope you feel better," Jessie told her.

Martha managed a small smile.

Jessie went back over to her brothers and sister. They needed to talk about the strange message on the board.

"Follow me," she whispered to her siblings, as they all left Room 214 and quietly closed the door.

"Do you think a ghost is really haunting these classrooms?" Violet asked as soon as they were out in the hallway.

Jessie was about to reply when the door opened behind them. They turned to see Martha leaving the classroom. She still had a strange look on her face and was walking quickly. As she slung her tote bag over her shoulder, a small piece of paper fell out, but she didn't stop. Jessie ran to pick it up, but by the time she had it in her hand, Martha had turned a corner. She was out of sight before Jessie could call to her.

Jessie looked down at the piece of paper. It was one of the bright-green business cards she had seen in Martha's bag.

"What is it?" Violet asked.

Jessie tucked the card into her back pocket and looked at her sister and brothers. "I'm not sure yet, but I'll show you over lunch. It's time for our break, isn't it?"

"It sure is," said Henry, checking his watch.

"I knew it was time for lunch even without a watch," Benny said, rubbing his tummy.

Violet checked the backpack she was carrying that held their food. Mrs. McGregor had made them each a brown bag lunch.

"I have an idea!" she said. "Let's find the lunchroom in this school! There has to be one, right? We can eat our sandwiches there, just like kids did in the old days."

Before long, they had found a door with a sign that said CAFETERIA.

The lunchroom looked a little bit like the one from the Aldens' own school. But the walls were covered in faded posters from the 1950s, showing black-and-white pictures of food. Jessie stood in front of a picture of a sandwich cut into neat triangles.

"It's a...cream cheese and pickle sandwich?" she said. She raised her eyebrows. "Yikes!"

The pickles in the picture were gray, and they didn't look very good to Jessie.

"I don't know," said Henry. "That sounds delicious! Except I would want olives instead of pickles."

"Really?" said Violet. "I can't imagine! The food was really weird in the fifties. Look!" She pointed to an old bulletin board with a tattered menu pinned to it.

"Today's lunch," she read aloud. "Milk, minced meat, mashed potatoes, beet relish, and tapioca pudding."

"*Beet* relish?" Benny asked. He wrinkled his nose. "I'm glad Mrs. McGregor made our lunch!" All the same, he was fascinated by the old menu and made Violet read the whole thing to him.

They sat down at one of the long tables. Benny opened his bag and let the contents spill out. He smiled when he saw Mrs. McGregor's famous turkey sandwich. She also had added carrots and a little tub of peanut butter. "My favorite!" Benny cheered, when he discovered the freshly baked chocolate-chip cookies.

The group was silent while they ate their sandwiches. Then Jessie pulled the small card from her pocket and stared at it.

"This is Martha's business card," she said. "I saw it in her bag when I got her water bottle. And...I think it's a clue!"

"What do you mean?" Henry asked.

"Well," Jessie replied, "the card says that Martha sells antique furniture! She has her own business."

"That would explain why she was looking at the desks so closely," Henry said. He remembered the first time they had met Martha.

"Wow," Violet said. "This school is filled with old furniture."

"Yes," Jessie continued. "I think Martha has been more interested in the furniture than in the restoration project. She must be looking for antiques to sell."

"Maybe *she* was the one who moved those desks into the basement," Henry said.

"And if she moved the furniture, then the Hawthorne School ghost didn't do it!" Bennie added.

"Exactly!" Jessie agreed.

Violet frowned. "That all makes sense," she said. "But why didn't Martha just tell us she was looking for antiques? Why all the sneaking around?"

Jessie crossed her arms and sighed. "That's a good question."

"And another thing," Violet added. "How did Martha know Watch's name?"

Chapter 6

Unusual Business

That evening, Grandfather made his famous spaghetti. He had spent an hour standing over the bubbling pot of sauce before he left it to simmer on the stove. Each time one of the children entered the kitchen to offer their help, he shooed them away. "It's a secret recipe!" he would say.

After dinner they made tapioca pudding for dessert. Benny had given Mrs. McGregor the idea after the Aldens returned from Hawthorne School. Benny told her all about the old menu. When he mentioned tapioca pudding, Mrs. McGregor took out a cookbook and showed him a picture of what looked like vanilla pudding filled with tiny, round blobs. Benny thought the pudding looked really funny, but he wanted to try it.

Now Mrs. McGregor set out the ingredients so the children could help make it. She showed them the package of tapioca, which looked like little white beads.

"Tapioca comes from the root of a South American plant called cassava," she explained.

"I think I've had tapioca before," Jessie said. "I had some bubble tea at the mall once, and there were little round pieces in it! They were soft, like jelly. It was weird but good!"

"Wow!" Benny said. Mrs. McGregor let him pour the beads into a measuring cup while she heated the milk for the pudding in a saucepan. Jessie cracked two eggs into a bowl and whisked them together.

"Violet," Mrs. McGregor said, "will you get the sugar, vanilla, and salt?"

After a few minutes, Mrs. McGregor added the rest of the ingredients to the milk.

Each of the Aldens took turns slowly stirring the mixture.

"Is it done?" Benny asked. He looked at the creamy pudding. It was now thick and filled with little translucent globes of tapioca.

"I think so," Mrs. McGregor told him. She poured the pudding into a bowl and covered it with wax paper. Benny opened the refrigerator door, and Mrs. McGregor set the sweet pudding inside.

While they waited for the pudding to cool, Mrs. McGregor finished cleaning the kitchen and Grandfather went to read in the next room. Benny, Jessie, and Violet gathered around Henry while he showed them what he'd found online.

"I wanted to know more about Martha's antique business," he said. "So I went to the website listed on her business card."

Benny pointed to a photo on the screen. "Those look like desks from Hawthorne School."

"They sure do," Henry said. "'Original antiques from a historic Silver City building,'" he read aloud. "'Will be in stock soon. No other dealer in town has these unique desks!'"

"Hmm," Violet said. "'No other dealer in town.' Do you think Martha has been making the school seem haunted so that nobody else would find out about those old desks?"

"It's a good theory," Jessie agreed. "She didn't want anyone to know she was interested in the desks. And she definitely didn't want other antique dealers to know about the school."

"That must be why she didn't want anyone to call the newspaper when we found the lesson on the old chalkboard," Henry added. "I'm sure she doesn't want the others to know about the furniture in the school."

Jessie grabbed her notebook off the kitchen counter and made some notes. "Martha is definitely a suspect," she said. "But then…she seemed really upset when she saw the message on the chalkboard in Room 214 today. I don't think she wrote that warning."

"Then who wrote it?" Benny asked.

Violet shrugged. "Maybe there's another suspect."

"What about Ansel?" Henry said. "He

keeps showing up with his camera right after each strange thing that happens at the school."

"Also, remember when he said that he wanted the school to stay exactly the way it is?" Jessie asked.

"Maybe he's trying to stop the renovation," Violet said. "But why?"

They were all silent for a moment as they thought. But nobody had any answers.

Henry closed the laptop and folded his hands in his lap. He leaned back in his chair.

"I think it's time to search for more clues," he said. "We should begin first thing Saturday morning."

Benny nodded. "But there's just one thing," he said.

"What is it?" Jessie asked.

"Can we have some tapioca pudding first?" Benny asked.

***

The Aldens were ready to leave the house two hours earlier than usual on Saturday morning. They'd asked Grandfather to take them to the Greenfield Public Library. The air was still crisp and cool when they got into the minivan.

"Hopefully we can get some answers today," Jessie said, as she tucked her notebook into her backpack.

Once they were in the library, Jessie pointed to the second-floor stairway that led to the Periodicals department.

"Let's check out old newspaper articles," she said. "Maybe we can find out more about the Hawthorne School ghost."

The Aldens found a computer station that they could use to look up digital copies of every issue published by the Silver City and Greenfield newspapers. Henry typed HAWTHORNE SCHOOL into the search box, and a dozen articles appeared on the screen. Jessie read the first one aloud.

"'Hawthorne School Bake Sale Next Friday,'" she said. "That was March 19, 1948."

"Mmm, a bake sale sounds good," Benny said.

Henry smiled and ruffled Benny's hair. "It sure does," Henry agreed.

"Here's another story from the 1940s,"

Jessie said, pointing to a headline that read "Hawthorne School Modernizes First-Floor Classrooms." "That must have been when they covered up that old blackboard."

Henry read the short article. "Interesting. But nothing about the Hawthorne School ghost."

They read a few more articles, one headlined "Fund-Raiser for Hawthorne School PTA" and another about the winner of an essay contest. But there was nothing about a principal who had been fired, and nothing at all about a curse or a ghost.

Benny yawned.

"I'm starting to wonder how anyone got the idea that Hawthorne School was haunted," Violet said. "Nothing interesting ever happened there!"

"Oh, I don't know," said Jessie, pointing to a headline. "According to this story, a photography darkroom was added to one of the classrooms in 1952. That's kind of cool."

"But it doesn't explain the ghost," Henry reminded them. He scrolled down to look at more stories.

"This one is sort of sad," he said. "It's about a Hawthorne student named Hyacinth Weaver," Henry said.

"Hyacinth," Violet repeated. "Like the kind of flower?"

Henry nodded. "The article says her parents owned Weaver's Flower Shop in Silver City. In spring 1955, Hyacinth had to get her tonsils taken out and missed the last week of school." He pointed to a black-and-white photo. It showed a young girl standing outside her parents' flower shop.

"That's *all*?" Jessie said. "She missed the *last week of school*?"

"But that's the best week of all!" Benny said.

Everyone laughed at that.

"There's one more article here, from later that summer," Jessie said. The headline read, "Hawthorne School's Doors Close for Good!"

"It says that the school wouldn't be reopening in the fall," Henry said, after reading the article. "Hawthorne School didn't have enough students anymore, so it was combined with Greenfield School. And since Greenfield had a bigger and newer school building, students had to go there instead of returning to Hawthorne."

Jessie wrote the date the school closed in her notebook: *June 10, 1955.*

"Well, that's it," she said. "Let's go meet Grandfather."

Grandfather was on the first floor of the library, standing next to the information center with a hardcover book tucked under his arm.

"Ready?" he asked.

The children nodded and walked with him to the minivan.

As they headed to Hawthorne School, Henry turned to his siblings.

"Do you think we've reached a dead end?" he asked them.

"It does seem strange that we didn't find any articles on the former principal," Violet said. "But I guess that means that story isn't true. And that there's no ghost."

"I thought we'd find something more interesting about the school," Jessie said.

"We only know about the bake sale," Benny added sadly. "And that was a long time ago."

When they reached the school, the Aldens climbed out of the minivan. They waved to Grandfather as he drove away.

"Let's check in with Bob," Henry suggested. "See where he needs us to help out today."

They looked up and down the hallways and in each classroom, but they couldn't find Bob.

"There's Ansel," Benny said, pointing down the hallway. "Maybe he knows where Bob went."

They watched as Ansel turned a corner and then was out of sight.

Violet gasped.

"What is it?" Jessie asked.

"I-I just remembered something from the articles at the library," Violet said. "I think I know where Ansel is headed. And it might be a clue!"

"How?" Henry asked.

"Follow me!" Violet said. And with that, she took off running in the direction Ansel had gone.

CHAPTER 7

Behind the Curtain

Henry, Jessie, and Benny ran after Violet. They caught up with her outside Room 108.

"In here!" she said.

Everyone followed Violet into the room. It was empty.

"Nobody's here," Jessie said. She spun around a few times to make sure she wasn't missing anything.

"Did Ansel vanish?" Benny asked as he peeked under a desk.

"Of course not," Violet said. "I know

where to find him." She walked over to a long curtain hanging in the corner of the room. It was made of dark, heavy velvet fabric, which she pulled back. Behind it was a tall, black pillar.

"What's that?" Benny asked, pointing at the pillar.

"It's a *door*," Violet said. "A special one."

The black pillar didn't look like a door at all. But Violet reached around it and found a small handle, which she pulled. The side of the pillar began to move, making a rolling noise.

"It *is* a door!" Jessie said with a gasp. "A curved, sliding door!"

The black door was a little bit like a revolving door in a store. They peered into what seemed to be a round closet.

"But what is it?" Henry asked.

"It's the door to the photography dark-room!" Violet exclaimed. "The one that was built in 1952! We read about it at the library this morning." Violet knew all about darkrooms. She had once taken a photography class and had used a door just like this one.

"So how do we get into the darkroom?" Jessie asked. This big, round black thing didn't look anything like a door. *No wonder nobody noticed it*, she thought.

"I'll show you," Violet replied. She stepped into the little round closet and motioned for the others to join her. "Now turn around and face the back," she said. As they did, she slid the curving door. The side of the closet that had been open to Room 108 now slid closed, and for a moment it was completely dark.

"Hang on," said Violet. She kept sliding the door until another room opened up— one on the other side. This room was lit by a glowing red light.

"I get it," Henry whispered. "The special round door lets you get to this red room without ever letting in the light from Room 108."

"Yes," Violet said. "Because the light would ruin the photographs."

"She's right!" said Ansel, his voice coming from the red-lit room. He was standing at a table and swishing a photograph around in a pan filled with liquid.

"Welcome to the darkroom," he said. "I've just printed a new photo. You can watch it develop."

The children went over to the table as Ansel picked up a pair of tongs. He used them to hold down photograph paper in a pan of processing solution. After a few moments in the solution, the blank paper changed to show a black-and-white image of Hawthorne School. The photograph was beautiful. Then Ansel dipped his tongs into the pan and pulled out the photograph. He moved it into another pan of liquid, then rinsed it in a third pan and clipped it to a line to dry.

Several other photographs hung alongside it. Each one was a different shot of the school. One was a close-up of an intricate woodcarving that Violet recognized from the banister in the front hallway. Another showed the overgrown yard behind the school. The bare trees looked like skeletons. Ansel's photos were all in just black and white, and they looked dark and mysterious.

"I had always heard about the darkroom,"

Ansel said. "So I looked for it the first time I came here with my dad."

"The night that we met you," Violet said.

Ansel nodded. "The equipment is in pretty good shape," he continued. "I've been printing my own photos here since the renovation started."

Jessie noticed the darkroom was neat and tidy. Ansel had taken special care to keep everything orderly.

"I'd always used a digital camera," Ansel explained. He pointed to a few different types of cameras on a shelf. "But then I started to experiment with traditional photography. This darkroom gave me the perfect opportunity to develop my own pictures."

"When we first met, you said you wanted to keep Hawthorne School the way it is," Jessie said.

Ansel furrowed his brow for a moment and swished another photograph around in the liquid. "I did say that, didn't I?"

"That's right," Henry said. "So you don't want Hawthorne School to be renovated into an art center?"

"That's not what I meant," Ansel replied. "I'm excited about having an art center. But I love how old and spooky the school is, and I was worried that the renovation would change that. I shouldn't have worried though...It's still as spooky as ever around here!"

The Aldens laughed along with him.

"And now," Ansel continued, "I have all of these photographs to show the school at its spookiest. I want to create a gallery to showcase them during the grand opening. It's important for people in Silver City to remember the history of old buildings like this one."

"That's a great idea," Henry said.

"Do you want to see some of the photos I've taken around the school?" Ansel asked.

The Aldens nodded enthusiastically. Ansel opened a drawer and pulled out a case. Inside was a binder full of black-and-white photos slid into clear plastic sleeves. The Aldens admired the photos. Ansel had captured the school's ghostly setting, but the images were also creative and beautiful.

"This one is very interesting," Violet said. She lifted the page to inspect the image.

"I like the way the locker doors are casting shadows in the hallway," Ansel replied.

In the photograph, all of the old locker doors were open. Violet noticed the lock dials were built into the doors. Their unique shape, combined with the lighting, made interesting shadows.

"Thanks for showing us your photos," Henry said. "And good luck getting everything done in time for the grand opening."

"Let us know if you need any help," Jessie added.

Ansel smiled. "I will."

Violet led everyone back through the small round closet and into Room 108. They sat down while Jessie took out her notebook.

"Now we know that Ansel isn't a suspect," Jessie said. She drew a line through Ansel's name in her notebook.

"And we know that a ghost didn't lock the door," Jessie said.

"Yes," Violet agreed. "When the volunteer was sweeping in here, she must not have known the darkroom door was there."

"Because it doesn't even look like a door!"

Benny said.

"Right," said Violet. "She left the room for a few minutes. When she returned, Ansel must have locked the door!"

"And he left later that night," Jessie added. "So the door was unlocked the next morning."

"So it wasn't a ghost!" Benny exclaimed. "It was just Ansel."

The Alden children looked at one another.

"This explains what happened in Room 108," Violet said. "But who is behind the warning on the chalkboard in Room 214?"

CHAPTER 8

An Unexpected Discovery

"Benny," Henry said, sweeping up a pile of dust, "will you hand me the dustpan?"

The Aldens were in the old auditorium, where their job was to sweep the floor. It needed to be clean for a fresh coat of paint. The art committee had asked local artists to design an emblem that would be painted on the floor. Bob had shown them a drawing of the design, which featured a beautiful *H*, *A*, and *C* for Hawthorne Art Center.

Cleaning the auditorium was one of the

Aldens' final volunteer tasks. They were impressed by the way the school was shaping up. Cobwebs had been brushed out of corners and crooks. Even tiny holes had been patched. And the walls were now painted a pristine white. Doorknobs were dusted and polished. Henry had even helped fix the flagpole. Now the flag waved and rippled in the wind, greeting everyone each day. Of course, some major work still needed to be done. The lockers had to be removed, and not all of the electrical work was finished. Even so, the school looked brighter and cleaner than ever.

But above and beyond the excitement around the renovations, the Aldens were looking forward to the grand opening party... and then participating in all of the programs the new art center offered!

Benny crouched down to hold the dustpan while Henry swept a heap of dirt into it.

"For being so old, the auditorium is in great shape," Henry said. He looked around and was impressed.

"Ansel made a good point," Violet said

from the stage. "Trying to keep the school's history alive in the renovation was a great idea. This building is so cool. It didn't need to be torn down!"

Behind Violet, Jessie bent down to wipe a smudge off the stage floor. She shook her head as she noticed muddy footprints leading offstage. Jessie wiped up the dirty tracks one by one.

The Alden children were so focused on their tasks that they didn't notice someone else was in the auditorium. But then they heard a voice.

"I can assure you," the woman said, "I am the first antique dealer to visit this school."

Jessie looked around and didn't see anyone. But she recognized the voice right away...It was Martha! Violet and Benny also looked around. Henry just shrugged.

"I bet the sound acoustics are really good in here," he explained. "After all, it is an auditorium, and the audience needs to be able to hear actors and musicians well."

"Where is she?" Benny asked.

"She's probably off in the wings somewhere,"

Jessie replied. "It sounds like she's talking on her cell phone."

Everyone went back to sweeping and wiping the floor. But they still heard Martha's conversation.

"I even scouted out the best pieces before the renovation started," Martha continued.

There was a long pause before she spoke again.

"No," she said firmly. "I've changed my mind about trying any more tricks to snap up the best pieces."

Another pause. Martha was listening to the person on the other end of the line.

"There's weird energy here," she finally said with a shaky voice. "I'll do my best to get good pieces, but from now on, I'm doing business fairly."

Martha said good-bye to her customer and ended the call. When she pulled back the curtain to the stage, she was startled to see the Aldens working.

"I didn't realize anyone was here!" she said.

"We're just finishing," Henry replied.

"Yes," Martha said as she looked around.

"You all have done a really nice job here. The new art center will be ready in no time!"

Jessie raised her eyebrows as a thought occurred to her.

"We heard you talking," she started. She pointed to the cell phone in Martha's hand. "And you said that you checked out the place before you started working here. When was that?"

Martha hesitated for a moment, as if not sure whether to tell the children the truth. Finally, she spoke. "It was the same night you were here. The night you met Bob," she admitted. "I found a flyer about the renovation project and came to the school to have a look."

Martha rummaged through her bag and pulled out a yellow piece of paper. She handed it to Henry. It was the same flyer Grandfather had found that led the Aldens to the Hawthorne School renovation.

"So," Henry said. He thought back to the first time they met Bob. "You knew who we were before we officially met on the first day of work. And you knew Watch too!"

Martha nodded and smiled.

"I was upstairs while you were walking through the classrooms," she said. "After you left for the playground, I slipped out the front door."

It all made sense now. Watch had been so jumpy that night because he sensed Martha's presence. And it also explained why the Aldens had the eerie feeling that someone was watching them. Someone was...Martha!

"Why did you keep it a secret?" Benny asked.

"I didn't want any other dealers to find out about all of the great antiques here," Martha replied.

Violet perked up as Martha explained her story. She remembered the rumor about furniture being moved in the school. Several volunteers thought the Hawthorne School ghost was responsible for desks and chairs that had been found in odd places. Now Violet thought that Martha could have done it.

"Did you move any of the furniture?" Violet asked.

"I did move some," Martha admitted. "I was hoping to save some of the best pieces, so I could be the first to bid on them at the auction. If someone else found them, they would be eager to bid before me."

The Aldens followed Martha to the edge of the stage. They all sat down and swung their legs over the ledge. Martha seemed less mysterious now. Over the past few weeks, she had simply been trying to find antique furniture. Jessie looked at a page in her notebook. Everything that Martha said seemed to add up. But she still had one last question.

"Martha, did you write the spooky message on the chalkboard in Room 214?" Jessie asked her.

Martha's eyes grew wide. "No!" she said. "I didn't write that message. I wish I knew who did though. It gives me the creeps." She crossed her arms and shivered.

The Aldens looked at one another. Martha had definitely acted strangely in the past. But now they knew her reasons. And something about the frightened look on her face made Jessie think that Martha was telling the truth when she said she hadn't written the spooky message. Jessie crossed her name off the list of suspects.

"We believe you," Jessie told Martha.

Henry and Jessie stood up and grabbed the brooms they had propped up against the wall. To their surprise, Martha also reached for a broom.

"It's time I started helping," she said, swishing the broom across the floor. Once she had a neat pile of dirt, Benny crouched down with his dustpan. In no time, they were nearly done cleaning the auditorium's floor.

"Thanks for your help," Violet told Martha.

Martha then grabbed a cloth and helped Jessie wipe scuffs and scrapes off the floor. They were busily cleaning when the auditorium door opened. They saw Mrs. Koslowski walking down the aisle. She was eyeing their progress, but she seemed like she had other things on her mind.

"Hi, Mrs. K," Henry said. "Can we help you with anything?"

"Hello," she replied. She waved quickly to the children. "No, I don't need any help."

Martha handed Jessie her dust cloth.

"I think we're done here," Martha said, looking at the spotless floor. "I'll take a walk with Hyacinth."

"Hyacinth?" Jessie asked. "Mrs. K's first name is...Hyacinth?"

"Hyacinth," Benny repeated. "Like the flower!"

"Lovely, isn't it?" Martha replied, smiling. "Her family owned Silver City's oldest florist. Have you seen Weaver's Flower Shop on Main Street? And Benny's right, she was named after her father's favorite flower."

Martha stepped off the stage and made her way to Mrs. Koslowski. The two of them walked out of the auditorium.

Jessie spun around to face her brothers and sister.

"Did you hear that?" she asked.

"Mrs. K is the girl from that newspaper article!" Henry exclaimed.

"The one who had her tonsils out and missed the last week of school!" Violet said.

"Wait a second..." Jessie flipped through her notebook, running her finger down each page as she scanned her notes. "That last week of school that she missed? It was also *the last week that Hawthorne School was ever open!*"

"That's true," Violet said. "All of the students had to go to Greenfield School that fall. I bet she missed her chance to say good-bye to her old classrooms. That might be why she's been wandering through the halls."

"Benny's right," Henry said. "The last week of school is always the best."

Jessie nodded. She remembered last June, when she and her friends had cleaned out their lockers. On the last day of school, they'd gathered their belongings to take home. That way, the school was clean and empty, ready for the next year.

"She didn't get to take her things home," Henry said. "They've been locked up here all these years."

Suddenly, Jessie looked up from her notebook. Her eyes lit up, as if she'd figured something out.

"Follow me," she said.

They followed Jessie back into the main school building. She raced up the stairs to the second floor. When she finally reached Room 214, she abruptly stopped.

As they entered the room, they saw the mysterious message still written on the chalkboard.

Stay away! Whoever dares unlock my secret will be sorry...

"Do you see?" Jessie asked. She excitedly pointed to the chalkboard.

"Yes!" Henry said. "Mrs. K must be trying to find her old locker. Her things have been locked away for sixty years!"

"So," Violet said. "Now we know."

Benny nodded. "Mrs. K wrote the mystery message!"

CHAPTER 9

Unlocking the Past

"It all makes sense!" Jessie exclaimed.

The Aldens continued to stare at the message Mrs. Koslowski had written on the chalkboard. The curvy, elegant handwritten letters spelled out the spooky words in the warning to stay away.

"Mrs. K must have wanted to find her things before someone else did," Violet said. "She was probably worried they would go into the trash. Then they would be gone forever."

Everyone agreed with Violet. Mrs. K wasn't

absentminded; she was just very focused on finding the things she had left in her locker all those years ago.

"She did a great job copying the writing we found on the chalkboard in Room 108," Henry said. He remembered that Mrs. K said the writing resembled her mother's penmanship. She must have used it as a guide when writing the note.

"We could just ask Mrs. K about it," Jessie suggested.

"We could help her find her things," Benny said.

Henry walked over to the old wooden table sitting in the middle of the room. He pulled out a chair and sat down.

"But every time we've seen her wandering the halls and ask her if she's looking for something, she's denied it," Henry said.

Jessie sat down at the table next to him.

"Maybe she doesn't want to bother anyone," Jessie said.

Violet and Benny also sat down at the table.

"If she doesn't find her things fast," Violet said, "it might be too late."

Henry nodded. "You're right," he said.

"And the renovation is in the final stage," Jessie added. "All the lockers will be torn out to allow room for the new gallery hall. All of the lockers will be thrown out...and everything in them!"

"We have to help Mrs. K," Violet said. "But how?"

"That's easy," Benny replied. "All we have to do is find the locked locker!"

They took turns high-fiving Benny for his clever idea. If they found the locker that had not been opened since the last day of school in 1955, they would surely find Mrs. Koslowski's hidden belongings.

"OK," Henry said. "Here's the plan."

He drew an outline of the school on a piece of loose-leaf paper.

"We'll have to divide into teams to tackle all of the lockers," he continued. "Jessie and Violet will take the first floor. Benny and I will take the lockers on the second floor. We'll meet here in an hour."

Henry pointed to a spot on the map directly in front of Room 108.

"Let's go," Jessie said, standing. "Let's find Mrs. K's long-lost things!"

Jessie and Violet headed downstairs to the lockers on the first floor. The red lockers looked old and dingy.

"Let's start with the top ones," Jessie suggested. The lockers were arranged in two rows, one on top of the other.

The sisters pulled the handle of each locker door. Every one opened easily.

"Now for the bottom row," Violet said.

After opening and closing each locker, the Alden sisters determined that Mrs. Koslowski's locker was not on the first floor.

Upstairs, Henry and Benny were not having much luck either. Each locker pulled open right away.

"It's getting late," Henry said. "We should head to Room 108."

Benny looked down the hallway at the unopened lockers. The second floor held several more rows than the first floor. Henry and Benny had not yet finished checking them.

"What if we never find Mrs. K's locker?"

Benny asked as they walked down the flight of stairs to the first floor.

"We'll just have to keep trying," Henry replied.

As they turned the corner, they saw Jessie

and Violet standing in front of Room 108. They were talking to Ansel.

"Look who we ran into," Jessie said.

"Ansel was just leaving the darkroom for the day," Violet added.

Henry asked Ansel about his project. Everyone wanted to know if he had found more interesting scenes to photograph.

"I've been playing more with the lighting and shadows from the open lockers," Ansel replied.

"Open lockers?" Jessie asked. "Did *all* of the lockers open?"

"As a matter of fact," Ansel replied, "One of them was locked."

"Mrs. K's locker!" Benny cheered.

The Alden children excitedly told Ansel about the old newspaper story and how they thought the locked locker was Mrs. Koslowski's.

"Where is the locker?" Henry asked.

Ansel explained that there was a short hallway on the second floor, off to the side of the main hall. It could be easily missed, if someone didn't know about it. The locked locker was in this nook.

"We must have missed it," Henry said. "We'll go check it out right now."

"And I'll find Mrs. K and bring her upstairs," Ansel said. "We'll all meet in front of the locker."

"Mrs. K will be so surprised!" Violet said.

Ansel went around the corner while the Aldens went up to the second floor, following Ansel's directions to the locker. Sure enough, there was a small hallway off the main hall. A few lockers lined the walls. Jessie took a deep breath and tried to open the very last one. It was locked!

"We found it!" Benny cried with delight.

"Now we wait," Jessie said.

A few minutes passed, but there was no sign of Ansel and Mrs. K. It was now late in the afternoon. They could see the sun dipping below the horizon out the window, and the light in the hallway was growing dim and shadowy. Jessie flipped on the light switch, but only a few bulbs glowed in the murky darkness. The other bulbs were cracked and broken. Henry had brought a battery-powered lantern to help look inside the lockers, and he held it up to give them some light, but it only helped a little bit. All around them in the gloomy hallway they could recognize the dark shapes and shadows from Ansel's photographs.

Violet shivered. "I can see why Ansel likes to photograph here," she said. "It sure is spooky."

Jessie nodded and hugged her arms to her chest.

"What if we're wrong about Mrs. K playing pranks?" Violet asked.

"What if there really is a ghost?" Benny continued.

Henry was about to tell Benny there was no such thing as a ghost at Hawthorne School. But then the Aldens heard the sound of a shut door rattling.

"What was that?" Violet asked.

A few moments passed. The door rattled again.

Jessie pointed to a dark doorway at the end of the hall. "It's coming from there," she said, her voice shaking a little.

The four of them were all thinking the same thing.

What if the legend of the Hawthorne School ghost was true after all?

CHAPTER 10

A Grand Opening

Just then, Benny stepped away from the lockers and stood in the center of the hallway. He crossed his arms.

"We can't be scared. We have to find Mrs. K," he said. "She's looking for something important."

"Benny's right," Henry said. "We have to see what's going on."

He led the way down the hallway, taking a second to peek into the open door of each classroom. All the rooms were empty. Finally, they reached the dark end of the hall...and the closed door.

Henry hesitated in front of the door.

"We have to open it!" Benny said. He stepped forward and placed his hand on the doorknob.

"For being so small, you sure are brave!" Violet told him.

Benny turned the knob and pulled it open, squeezing his eyes closed as he did. If there was a ghost, he didn't want to see it!

"Thank goodness!" cried Mrs. K, who stood with Ansel and Bob behind the door. "We came up the back stairs, but this door wouldn't open!"

Jessie let out a sigh of relief as the adults came into the hallway.

"I understand you have something to show me?" Mrs. K asked.

"Yes!" Benny exclaimed. "Come on!"

"Wait a moment," said Mrs. K. "Let me sit down for a moment. I need to tell you all something."

Bob found a chair from one of the classrooms and brought it over to Mrs. K.

She gently sat down. She removed her glasses and blinked a few times. Then she pulled a tissue out of her pocket and nervously began cleaning the lenses of her glasses.

"I'm terribly sorry," she started. "I had no idea my little message would get this out of hand. Everybody was talking about the Hawthorne ghost, and I thought the warning might buy me a little time to find my things."

She put her glasses back on. Mrs. K appeared to be more bashful than usual. She took a deep breath and then fiddled with her glasses again.

"We know you were searching for your old locker," Henry said. "You must have left something in there."

"You had to leave school to have your tonsils taken out," Jessie continued.

"But then the next year, you went to Greenfield School," Violet said.

"So you never got your things from your locker!" Benny finished.

"Yes...yes, it's all true," Mrs. K said.

The Alden children watched as Mrs. Koslowski relaxed. Bob brought her a bottle of water. She slowly sipped it.

"A week before I went into the hospital, my grandmother gave me a bracelet—a token of good luck," Mrs. K finally said. "It was gold with tiny amethyst crystals. My birthstone... and also my grandmother's birthstone. I was so proud of it I brought it to school to show my friends! But then... I forgot it."

"Hyacinth explained that the bracelet is very precious to her," Bob said. "Not because of its cost, but because it came from her grandmother!"

Mrs. Koslowski nodded. She touched her wrist, as if she was stroking an imaginary piece of jewelry.

"I'm sure the volunteers will understand," Jessie said. "Maybe you could tell them your story."

"And then they'll know there is no such thing as the Hawthorne ghost!" Benny added.

Mrs. K brightened. "Bob," she said. "Do you think you could gather the volunteers? I'd like to apologize to them!"

Everyone smiled. Bob said he would call a volunteer meeting for the following day. Mrs.

K would have her chance to tell them how sorry she was for scaring them during the renovations.

Henry turned to Mrs. K. "Now," he said. "Let's get your things."

Mrs. K jumped to her feet. She followed Henry as he led the way down the hallway. She had a spring in her step.

"This is it," Jessie said, pointing to the shut locker. She spun the dial a few times. Then she asked Mrs. Koslowski for the combination.

"I'm not sure I remember it," Mrs. K replied. "I didn't even remember my locker was here."

She called out a few numbers as Jessie turned the dial. Each combination turned out to be wrong. The locker was still shut tight.

"Did you use a special date as the combination?" Henry asked. "For my school locker, I use the day, month, and last two digits of the year we met Grandfather. That way, I always remember it."

"Yes, that's right," Mrs. Koslowski replied. "My grandmother's birthday. Try this, Jessie…"

She recited three more sets of numbers. This time, the dial clicked, and the locker opened. Mrs. Koslowski reached inside and pulled out a small box. Opening it, she revealed a beautiful, sparkling gold bracelet with soft purple gemstones. Violet helped Mrs. K clasp it around her wrist.

"What else is in there?" Benny asked.

"Let's see," she replied. She reached into the locker again and pulled out some old

school supplies and a pencil case. Everyone chose an item to examine.

"It's like we opened a time capsule!" Jessie exclaimed.

She was holding one of Mrs. K's old school folders. On the front, several animated characters were cheerfully giving the thumbs-up sign.

"Look at these," Henry said as he turned over a few coins in his hand. Although old, the coins were shiny and bright from being tucked away in the dark locker.

Mrs. K turned to Benny. "Oh dear," she said, seeing the small plastic horse he was holding. "That's a toy from my favorite TV show. I'd forgotten all about these things. Finding them now is like taking a trip down memory lane!"

Under a few schoolbooks, they discovered an old newspaper that had been stashed away in the locker. The Alden children took turns reading the current events from 1955.

Everyone was excited that Mrs. K had finally found her belongings. Bob even suggested featuring them in the new display case.

"What a wonderful idea," Mrs. K replied.

Violet nodded enthusiastically. "This way," she said, "everyone who visits the art center will know what school was like in the fifties."

The Alden children knew that Grandfather would arrive soon to pick them up. As they said good night to Bob, Ansel, and Mrs. K, she turned to them one last time.

"Thank you!" she called. And then she descended the back staircase and was out of sight.

***

Grandfather and the Alden children stood on the stone steps of the new Hawthorne Art Center. They looked up at the old building with astonishment. It was hardly the spooky school they had found months earlier while running their weekend errands. In fact, although the sun was setting, the area was lit up. Several street lamps had been added to the parking lot, and small lanterns lined the path to the front door. Inside the building, all of the broken lights had been fixed. The old school glowed brightly. The renovations were complete.

Grandfather opened the newly painted red door and ushered the children inside. A large banner in the entrance hall read, GRAND OPENING PARTY!

Henry looked around. "Wow!" he said. "Everything looks great. It's like a brand-new building."

Violet gazed up at the grand trophy case, now without the cobwebs. The old trophies had been polished and looked beautiful.

"Yes," she said. "And it still has all of the details that made Hawthorne School so special."

Bob spotted the Aldens and welcomed them to the party. As Grandfather chatted with him, the Alden children continued to walk through the art center. They marveled at how much it had changed.

They came to Room 108. Instantly, they recognized the photographs hanging on the walls inside the room. They were the black-and-white pictures Ansel had taken before the renovations were finished. They turned out to be spooky and artistic—just as he had hoped. Violet found a sign-up sheet for photography lessons. She put her name on the list. She couldn't wait to start taking her own photographs.

Next door, the antique chalkboard was now behind a plastic case. The old-fashioned lessons and curvy handwriting were preserved for everyone to see.

They walked upstairs to find that the hall was now a gallery space. There was room for drawings and sculptures to be displayed.

"It's a good thing Mrs. K found her things when she did," Jessie noted. "She almost lost them forever."

As the others nodded, they heard someone walk up behind them.

"And I owe it all to you," Mrs. K said.

The children turned to see Mrs. Koslowski. They noticed right away that she was wearing her purple and gold bracelet. After a few minutes of catching up, Henry asked if she ever spoke to the other volunteers. He wondered if she'd had the chance to tell them about the strange message she wrote on the chalkboard.

"Oh yes," she said. "Bob called a meeting

for the next day. I put the Hawthorne ghost rumor to rest once and for all!"

Everyone was thrilled with the good news. They said good-bye to Mrs. K and headed back downstairs to look for Grandfather. He was still standing with Bob. As they joined them, Ansel and Martha also approached.

"Your photographs are wonderful," Violet told him. "We saw them hanging in Room 108."

"Thanks!" Ansel replied. "You should see the darkroom. It's all fixed up and ready for photography students to use."

Violet smiled, knowing she would soon have the chance to test it out herself.

Jessie turned to Martha. "How is your antique business?" she asked.

Martha couldn't wait to tell them all about it. When the furniture finally went to auction, she was the first bidder. All of the furniture sold quickly.

"Except," she said, "for a very special piece. I saved this for myself…"

Martha pulled out her cell phone and showed them a photo of the old clock.

"It's now fixed and works perfectly!" she said.

Bob turned his attention to the children. "What do you think of the new art center?" he asked.

"It's perfect," Jessie replied.

"There's just one thing missing," Benny said.

Bob looked puzzled. "What's that?" he asked.

"The snack tent!" Benny replied.

Everyone laughed.

Turn the page to read an exclusive sneak peek
of the newest Boxcar Children Mystery!

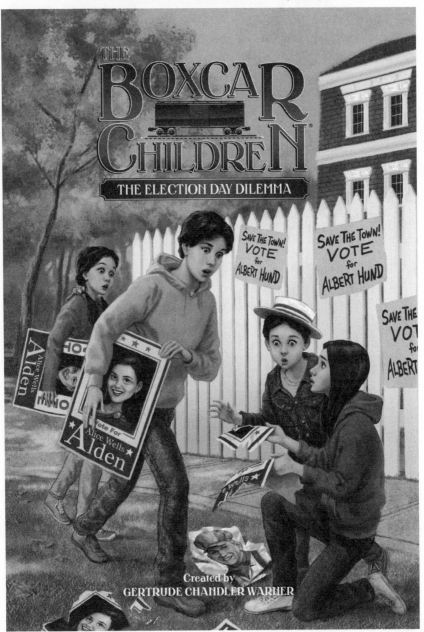

PB ISBN: 9780807507223, $5.99

CHAPTER 1

Not a Good Sign

"There's the sign for Appleville ahead!" Six-year-old Benny Alden called out from the back seat of his grandfather's car. "I see the big apple on it! We're almost there."

"Good. I was afraid we'd be late for Cousin Alice's speech," Benny's sister, twelve-year-old Jessie said. "It's so exciting that she might become the mayor of Appleville."

Henry, who was fourteen and the oldest of the Alden children, checked his watch. "We should make it with plenty of time."

"I can't wait to see Soo Lee. We haven't seen her in a while," Benny's other sister, ten-year-old Violet said. Soo Lee was Cousin Alice and Cousin Joe's daughter. She was about Benny's age and the Alden children always had fun when she was with them.

Suddenly a *thump, thump, thump* sound came from beneath the car. The car veered to the right as if it was going to go off the road. Grandfather struggled to bring the vehicle under control. Watch, the Aldens' dog, yelped and crouched down on the seat. Everyone held their breath. When the car came to a stop, Violet cried, "What happened?"

Grandfather gave a sigh. "A tire blew out. It happens sometimes. Everyone all right?"

Jessie checked on Violet and Benny before she replied, "We're fine."

"We may be fine, but I'm not sure Appleville is," Violet said, pointing to a trembling figure out the window.

The car had come to stop right underneath the Appleville sign. Usually the sign welcoming people to the town had an image of a big yellow apple with a smiley face on it and the slogan, "Appleville: A Happy Place!" in large red letters.

This time it was different. "Something is wrong with the sign," Benny said.

"Someone has been painting on it," Jessie said. A large black bird with a red head had been painted to look like it was flying over the apple, which now had a frown painted over the smile. The word "happy" had been crossed out and a new word painted above it.

"It says "cursed" doesn't it?" Benny asked. Benny was just learning to read. "It says, "Appleville: a Cursed Place!"

"Yes, and there's more," Henry said. "Someone painted on the bottom of the sign too."

Violet's voice was shaky when she read the words aloud. "It says, "Move Away! You've been warned!"

Benny hunched down in the seat. "I don't know if I want to go to Appleville anymore. Why would Alice want to be mayor of a cursed town?"

"Someone is just playing a trick," Jessie

said, putting her arm around Benny. "A town can't be cursed."

"It's terrible that someone ruined their sign," Violet said.

"It's also illegal," Grandfather added. "Whoever did it is defacing someone else's property."

"I wouldn't want to paint that kind of bird," Violet said. "It's very ugly." Violet was a good artist. She liked to draw and paint birds and animals.

"What kind of bird is it?" Benny sat up and looked out the window again, feeling a little better.

"It's some type of vulture," Henry said. "See how small its head looks compared to its body? Vultures don't have feathers on their heads so they look strange compared to other birds."

"I wonder why the town hasn't fixed the sign," Jessie said. "It won't make people want to visit Appleville."

"We can ask Alice and Joe, but first we'll have to do something about the tire." Grandfather opened the car door.

"How far are we from Joe and Alice's house? Can we ride our bikes there?" Violet asked. The Alden children's bikes were secured to the bike rack on their grandfather's car.

"It's not very far, but it's getting dark and it's chilly out." Grandfather took his phone out of his pocket. "I'll just call someone to come out and change the tire."

"I can change it," Henry said, "We have a spare tire in the trunk."

"I'll help," Jessie said.

Grandfather thought for a moment and then nodded his head. "It's nice to have such handy grandchildren."

While Henry and Jessie were changing the tire, Violet and Benny got out of the car with Watch to look around. The only house they saw was set back across a field of dead grass. Next to the house were rows of small trees. Behind the house was a forest.

"Those woods looks like where we found our boxcar," Violet said. After their parents had died, the Alden children were scared to go live with their grandfather, not knowing him and fearing he was mean. They had run away and found an old boxcar to live in until their grandfather found them, and they realized he wasn't mean after all.

"It looks spookier than where we had our boxcar." The trees behind the house were tall and spindly and crowded close together. Bushes with dark leaves grew underneath the trees so it was hard to see very far into the forest. Benny shivered and glanced back up at the sign and the vulture. "I don't know if I want to wait out here."

"It's only spooky because it's getting dark," Violet said, though she felt a little uneasy too.

"That's a creepy, old house," Benny said. "I wonder if anyone lives there." The house hadn't been painted in a long time. Some of the shutters hung crookedly from the windows.

"I think it's empty. There aren't any lights on and there are weeds all over the yard." A flash of red caught Violet's eye. "Look! Maybe someone does live there. There's a woman in a red jacket."

An older woman with white hair wearing a red coat stood by a side porch looking up at the house.

Violet waved and called, "Hello!"

The woman didn't turn around. Instead she walked around the corner of the house until she disappeared from Benny and Violet's view.

"That's strange," Violet said. "She didn't even wave at us."

"We're done!" Henry called.

"We just need to put away the tools and then we can be on our way," Jessie added.

Watch began to growl. "What's wrong, boy?" Benny asked. Watch growled again and then stalked forward, crouched low to the ground.

"He sees a dog over at the house." Violet pointed to a big shaggy brown dog staring at them from the steps of the house.

Watch crept toward the other animal. "Watch, come back!" Violet called. But Watch didn't listen. He leaped forward and dashed off into the tall grass between the car and the house.

The big dog saw Watch running toward him. Even though Watch was much smaller, the shaggy animal acted scared of the little terrier. He turned and ran away into the woods before Watch could reach him.

"Watch!" Violet yelled.

Henry and Jessie heard Violet and hurried over to her and Benny.

"WATCH!" Henry shouted. Watch stopped and looked back over his shoulder.

Jessie whistled. "Watch, come back!" This time Watch listened. He bounded back to the car wagging his tail.

"It's a good thing you didn't get lost," Benny scolded the dog.

"Let's go," Grandfather said. "We should make it just in time."

Everyone piled back in the car. As they drew close to town, they passed another sign. This one showed a smiling white-haired man wearing overalls and a train conductor's hat. Words across the top of the sign read "Charlie Ford for Mayor. Vote for Charlie and help Appleville chug into the future!"

"That's funny," Benny said. "Towns can't chug like trains. I thought Alice was going to be mayor."

"Only if she gets elected," Jessie explained.

"Charlie Ford must be another candidate who is running against her. She'll have to get more votes than he does to win the race."

Benny laughed. "It's funny to say Mr. Ford is *running* against Alice. It sounds like they have to race around a track to see who wins."

"That would be fun to watch but not a good way to decide who is in charge of a town," Henry said.

"I like Mr. Ford's hat," Benny said. "I wish I had a train conductor hat."

"Mr. Ford is lucky no one painted on his sign," Violet said. "I still can't believe someone ruined the town sign."

Benny wished Violet hadn't brought up the Appleville sign. He didn't want to think about a curse.

GERTRUDE CHANDLER WARNER discovered when she was teaching that many readers who like an exciting story could find no books that were both easy and fun to read. She decided to try to meet this need, and her first book, *The Boxcar Children*, quickly proved she had succeeded.

Miss Warner drew on her own experiences to write the mystery. As a child she spent hours watching trains go by on the tracks opposite her family home. She often dreamed about what it would be like to set up housekeeping in a caboose or freight car—the situation the Alden children find themselves in.

While the mystery element is central to each of Miss Warner's books, she never thought of them as strictly juvenile mysteries. She liked to stress the Aldens' independence and resourcefulness and their solid New England devotion to using up and making do. The Aldens go about most of their adventures with as little adult supervision as possible—something else that delights young readers.

Miss Warner lived in Putnam, Connecticut, until her death in 1979. During her lifetime, she received hundreds of letters from girls and boys telling her how much they liked her books.